Panspermian Earth

David Kernot

Published by David Kernot, 2013.

This is a work of fiction. Similarities to real people, places, or events are entirely coincidental.

PANSPERMIAN EARTH

First edition. October 19, 2013.

ISBN: 979-8230114437

Written by David Kernot.

Table of Contents

To my wife, Olivia, who lets me dream, always!

INTRODUCTION

If you believe that we are not alone in the universe, if you believe that there is more to life than what just appears on the Earth, then I hope this series of seven connected stories will make you think. At one level this is a story about the fight between Gaia and her sister Halaconia in apocalyptic worlds, but in many ways it is a reflective piece of when people look up at the stars and wonder if there is any sense to the madness that is our lives, and they might wonder if perhaps we are not alone in the universe but part of a bigger mosaic of life. I hope you like it.

David Kernot

Author

June 2013

Editors Note: In 2025, four further short stories were added to this edition around the theme of panspermia and the concept of terraforming Venus

PART I: OCEANIA

GAIA'S VIRUS

I AM OCEANIA, AND GAIA was my eldest sister. In the days before the Apocalypse, before celestial telepathy was as effective as it is now, she caught the virus.

I didn't know. As sisters, we were worlds apart. I have only a recounting of what happened from our mother.

It was during the 'Hello from Earth Pulse' — another thing that wasn't her fault — when the plague struck hardest. Momentarily, all eyes were upon her. The repercussions, however, were lasting.

I ask myself what I would have done in her situation? How could she have known the ramifications of her actions back then? Would anyone have done it differently? Ultimately, I understand her motives, even if genocide wasn't the answer. It didn't change much.

It is important to tell the story the way it was told to me, so you understand why I did what I did, and why I'm not to blame for what happened, any more than Gaia. We were sisters. Everything else was merely coincidental.

After Gaia passed, my mother recounted everything. I was old enough then to comprehend, although I don't know how mother gained so much detail. I expect that there are things about the cosmos I am unaware of, so forgive me for telling it this way, but it is insightful about the threat within us all.

Gaia raised her core temperature and bled out as a way of cleansing herself, but she couldn't undo the damage. They discovered the self-regulating, symbiotic effects of the virus later. If they had known the virus was equally important to us as we to it, then Gaia wouldn't have acted that way.

After she passed, the celestial bodies in my region grew frustrated over the 'Hello from Earth Pulse'. It was as though the pulse itself contained a form of self-assimilation to trigger cells within us. Our bacteria grew, then mutated. And when pieces of Gaia arrived — small virus-strewn fragments — and landed within our skins, infections began. Like Gaia, we suffered. No one was sure if the cause was Gaia's self-destruction, or worse; whether the virus had the intelligence to exit her body and travel the cosmos searching for new hosts.

It infected me first. Gaia is my nearest sister, after all. I formed an idea of what I was on the inside, became more aware, and sensed the ebb and flow of my life's blood as if it were a tide.

I did nothing. I let Gaia's virus spread and run its course.

I believe in the value of learning from what has gone before. I wanted to act, lash out, and fight like Gaia did. Instead, a passive aggression ate me up. And while I feel different inside now, I must take solace in the fact there is a piece of my sister within me, and that we are all connected somehow.

But even so, the virus grows...

GAIA'S LEGACY

The Earth shook. Alan pulled himself from his small bunk and raced outside into a new dawn. By the time he stood on the launch pad next to the scramjet, *Andromeda*, the ground had stopped shaking. Tsunami was his first thought; they were vulnerable this close to the shore. Out across the Equatorial Sea, poisonous brown scum floated on the choppy surface, a constant reminder of the world's failure.

He ran down onto Europa Base's beach, past the dinghy, but everything looked the same: half-dead palm trees, and the tall, buckled structures of the space launch site. He wiped his brow. Had nobody else heard it? He needed to wake Lisa, in case there was trouble. He strode back toward the small circle of huts that formed the scientific camp's sleeping quarters.

"Dr. Derringer!"

Alan stopped. He turned to face one of their security team. "Did you feel that?"

"Yes. The national seismic center confirmed it was a size 3.8 tremor, about 50 klicks behind us into the hills."

"No tsunami threats then?"

"No, but strangely enough about thirty quakes hit at the same time all across the Earth."

"Thirty?"

"Yep, and there are no reports of damage anywhere. It's like someone drove a great rumbling truck across the world and then vanished."

Alan nodded. It had sounded like a truck rumbling along. "Bizarre. I suppose I'll find out more soon enough. I'll be back at Meridian City today. I'll check out the *Andromeda*, just to be sure." The lie came easily enough; truth was he dreaded climbing aboard. "No issues last night?" asked Alan.

"No, but trouble comes in waves. I suspect your launch today will bring the apocos back, that or the quake."

Alan frowned. "Apocos? Apocalypse survivors?"

The guard nodded.

"So, how dangerous is it here?"

"They're not that much trouble; they come for the tech mainly, food, or anything else they can get their hands on."

"Are there really as many as the reports say?"

"There are about twelve hundred survivors. They live in a cave about 20 klicks up the coast."

Alan thought about it. "That's a lot of people. Sure they won't try to invade?"

The guard shrugged.

Alan laughed. The man was a veteran. "I take it you're staying then, Master Sergeant?"

"You bet."

Alan stepped onto the launch pad uneasily, and walked around the scramjet, checking *Andromeda's* panels and external structure. He stopped at the highly polished golden plaque covered in engraved symbols; the Earth in relation to the Sun, Earth's place in the universe, and a naked man and woman. It was standard fare for all spacecraft since the 1970s Voyager Space Probes. *Andromeda* should have tasted the cold of deep space, with him as a pilot. But they ended up serving in different ways: Alan as microbiologist, and *Andromeda* as a cargo vessel.

"Do you miss it, Dr. Derringer?"

Alan turned. He had forgotten the guard. "Miss it?"

"Space travel. Were you *Andromeda's* pilot?"

Alan nodded. "Long time ago."

"Ever want captain her again?"

Alan took a deep breath. "Sometimes." The word tasted false. All the time would have been too much of an admission, especially if he could have changed what had happened. "Mostly, I'm happy to let the AI autopilots do their job." He thought about *Andromeda's* sister ship, *Centaurus*, long since destroyed, and sighed. He looked down at his shaking hands and realized it might as well have been yesterday. At least *Andromeda* had survived. "At least we don't get the same human errors."

"So an AI would have saved the crew's lives?" The guard knew his history, and why wouldn't he?

Alan shrugged. His chest tightened, and his voice caught with emotion. "Perhaps, I don't know. Sometimes we think we're unbreakable. Age teaches you otherwise." He looked up at the blackened ruins nearby. "This was to be our push to Mars, and then it all stopped."

"But they came to us."

"The signal from the Drake Outpost?" It was true the listening station on the dark side of the moon heard something; an abnormal alpha transmission, but alien life?

"Yes, sir. They found us."

Alan took a deep breath and breathed easier. "I think we may have found them. Perhaps because they noticed one of our probes, or heard all our EM radiation and noise."

"So they're coming to shut us up?"

Alan laughed. "Perhaps. That's what the guys on the Drake Outpost will discover. Turn your TV's down, there are too many reruns of *Leave it to Beaver* and *I Love Lucy* propagating across the universe."

"You're funny, Dr. Derringer."

"Call me Alan."

"I don't know if I could, sir, but I'm Geoff. We'll see each other again, I've got eight months before I get down to Mawson City."

Alan thought about the stray shots, and the missing scientific gear, and decided that Geoff was a typical soldier and loved his job. "So what's it like at Mawson City?"

"It's nice. All that land and fresh water, plus there's the shrinking ice pack in the center. I've heard it's better than your continent. What do they call it? The dry ring colony? Miserably cold North Pole Sea one minute, ice the next. Give me the South Pole any day."

Alan laughed over the world's choices. He'd been a teenager twenty years ago, when twenty billion people tried to crowd the poles. "Better than here. What is it at the equator now, a mild 115 degrees? But you might be right. I might take Leece down to Mawson City one day. Never been down to Antarctica."

"So when are you and Dr. Moran going to tie the knot?"

"Leece and I?" That surprised him. They weren't even dating. "She's my research assistant."

"If you say so."

Alan smiled. "Are my feelings that obvious?"

The guard nodded. "It's written all over her face too. Marry her."

He chuckled. "That's good to know, but we're not dating."

The guard leaned back and frowned. "Why in heavens not?"

Alan shrugged. "We're always together as it is. I think there's an understanding between us, but it never seems to be the right time to talk about."

"Don't let her get away."

"I don't intend to." Alan reached up and unlatched a small panel on the scramjet and pressed a button. A large door panel pushed out from the craft's smooth surface. He unhooked it and then stepped back as it lowered to become a ramp.

Alan forced a smile and pushed back his discomfort at climbing inside *Andromeda*. "I'll go in and check the systems."

"Don't want to play second fiddle with the AI?"

"Something like that."

"Sit your girl up in the flight cabin, I hear the view is exceptional. Pop the question, then."

Alan felt for the ring box in his pocket. "About living together, sure. As to the rest, you never know."

"I'll come back and see you both off."

Alan nodded and stepped inside. He went over the checks again and again, like he had before they left Meridian City. He couldn't afford a repeat of *Centaurus*. Leece would be on the flight. He broke into a cold sweat thinking about her lovely skin burning like parchment... no, he couldn't think about that.

AS LISA STEPPED FROM the research hut, Alan realized that as much as he hated this place, the lack of people was a blessing.

"It's not too bad here," she said, sinking her toes into the sand. "At least, it won't be when your oxygen producing bacteria clean up these poisoned oceans. What are you going to call your recent find?"

"I thought I could name it after you."

She laughed mischievously. "We *could* stay, and I'll work on that *all-over* tan for you."

He laughed back. "I've calculated that at the rate the bacteria are multiplying, the sea could be back in balance within three to five years. It might be possible to rebuild a decent colony in the equatorial region."

"We could wait it out here," she said.

"Sitting and watching you get an all-over tan would make an interesting study." A warm glow lit his cheeks.

"Last chance, mister? Bikini top goes away until our next visit."

She had that look that Alan loved.

"Sadly, as romantic as a hut by the sea is, I suspect I will have to report to Bill in Meridian as soon as possible."

"Later then?"

"Absolutely. The bacteria will need monitoring."

The scramjet's engines started up the beach.

"Let's go then," said Alan.

"Did you send the report to Bill?"

"Err, yes." He knew Bill wouldn't be happy to report their findings. "He will be hopping mad when he reads it. I said the tests failed, and I switched the results."

"What? Serious? We will keep the results from the northern government?"

"Yes, and the southern government. I'm taking samples to Meridian. We'll classify it so they won't have access to the data. Nobody outside the team needs to know while the bloom here is healthy and continues to grow. Until we can be sure there won't be any negative effects from spawning the bacteria elsewhere."

He gave Lisa's hand a squeeze as they walked towards the jet. She squeezed back. He wondered if he should ask her to marry him on the trip back home. Perhaps at the New Year's celebrations.

Geoff, the Master Sergeant, was waiting at the scramjet. He saluted and then grinned at Alan.

"There are still two chairs in the front for you, Captain, if you needed a better view." The guard winked.

Alan nodded, and his cheeks burned. But as he stepped inside, uneasiness returned.

Alan's cheeks were cool by the time he locked the door and sat, but his nervousness had escalated.

Leece leaned in when they were seated. "Captain? What was that all about?"

He forced a smile. Inside *Andromeda*, it didn't seem funny, and his palms went sweaty. He rubbed them on his jumper. "I'll tell you... maybe once we're stable, after launch."

"You don't like flying, do you?"

He shook his head.

"You know it's the safest form of transport," she said and squeezed his hand. "Don't worry, I'll keep your mind off things." She giggled.

He closed his eyes and nodded. It would be harder than she could imagine.

MEMORIES UNFOLDED FROM a lifetime ago...

On the launch pad at Europa Base, he felt *Centaurus'* vibrations inside *Andromeda*. His radio squawked...

Captain Melanie Grayson said, "Good luck, *Andromeda*."

Alan barely contained his excitement, "Back at you, *Centaurus*."

"See you on the dark side of the moon."

Base Command: "*Centaurus* launched."

"God speed, *Centaurus*." Alan's voice was barely a whisper.

Seconds later he felt *Andromeda's* lift and braced himself for the culmination of his dreams.

Base Command: "Problem with *Centaurus*—"

Base Command: "Aborting mission... *Andromeda*, brace, brace..."

Alan tensed. *Centaurus'* impact wrenched Alan from his seat, sent him across the cockpit into the far wall. He remembered his arm snapping, his shoulder dislocating...

Everything went blank.

"ALAN, WE'RE HERE."

Lisa shook him and slowly, he forced himself upright.

"Alan, wake up, this is the best part, the view of Meridian."

"Okay, awake." He rubbed his eyes and looked out the scramjet's projected window image. His hand went to his shoulder, feeling the scar tissue and the pin. He took a breath, and pushed away the memories of

Centaurus and his fiancée, Captain Melanie Grayson. The tall domes of the polar ringed city sparkled, stood proud amongst the tundra.

Alan only wished that there were more accommodating places to live. High world temperatures, oil-contaminated water, desalination plant, toxic salt waste, a slough of poisoned, radiated lands from power plants, all spread across the oceans. The Poles, with their fresh, untapped water, and most tolerable temperatures, were all the globe had left to offer. Unless the bacteria could change that.

Tonight, he decided. He smiled. "Come with me to New Year's in Meridian Square?"

"Really?"

"Yes, something I want to tell you."

"Ooh, mysterious. Tell me now." She grinned.

He grinned back at her, and the muscles in his cheeks tightened. "Something I want to *ask* you then."

"Oh, sounds *very* important," she said, mimicking his serious tone.

Alan smiled. She *had* to know, everything about her screamed she knew. He took a deep breath. "Tonight, then?"

"I wouldn't miss it."

He took a breath.

The scramjet shook.

"That's strange," said Lisa, sitting up straighter. "Did you feel that?"

"I did." He leaned forward and looked at the window display.

"Shuttle 141, move to a holding pattern," barked a metallic voice from the front speaker. "We have a problem with the landing pad."

Alan looked out. A crack opened up in the tarmac, growing wider and wider. White condensed steam puffed out. "Leece." A building shook and then collapsed. The cracks widened, and the building vanished.

Gaseous fire belched from the ice near the landing pad, and a rift opened in the permafrost. Lava spewed into the air. He punched an override code into the keypad on his armrest and spoke into a recessed microphone. "Initiate climb to 5000 feet!"

The jet rose, shaking as it travelled through pockets of scorching air.

"How did you do that?"

"They gave me access," he said.

Alan looked below. Dozens of vents opened up around Northern Alliance cities. The lava spread. In minutes it covered the settlement. Buildings collapsed. Some leaned and then fell into the pool of grey-red molten lava. Steam bloomed from the icy sea when it quenched the flowing lava. He grabbed the phone from the seat console and dialed Bill.

"Bill, what the hell's happening?"

"I'm at home... with the family... everything around me is shaking," yelled Bill.

"Can you take cover?"

"I don't know? It's my girl's fourth birthday tomorrow — she's with us now — and all the cakes and candy bags are shaking. I don't know how it will go, if this all—"

The phone went dead. "Bill?"

More silence followed.

"Bill?"

Below him, the city erupted in a flash of red lava. Like a river it spread, covered Meridian and swept everything up in its path. Everything vanished in a few blinks of the eye. He felt numb, lost for words.

Bill and his family; three daughters were down there, the rest of the team too. All his friends; everybody he had ever known. Cold clawed within him. He couldn't fathom what had just happened, and he shook his head. It was indescribable, beyond comprehension. How could an entire population vanish? He felt ill and wanted to vomit, but as he bent over and stared at his shoes, nothing came except tears.

He wanted to say something, but words wouldn't form.

Lisa sat rigid, staring at the window image, hands over her mouth, screaming into the silence.

He touched the intercom, pressed some arm-pad keys. "Climb and fly to Mawson City?"

Leece turned to him and croaked. "The South Pole? We can't leave."

He understood her logic. Stay, look for survivors, do something. "There's nothing we can do here, Leece. There's nobody left."

She nodded and closed her eyes in tears.

Alan took a deep breath and exhaled slowly. The scramjet's shaking added to his uneasiness. He unclipped his seat belt, stood up, and placed his hand on her shoulder. "There are people down in the south, trauma therapists... it won't be long until—"

The craft shook, and he gripped the chair. Geeze! He leaned into Leece, "I will sit up front with the AI. Coming?" He held out his hand and waited.

The craft lurched sideways and Alan sailed across the cabin. He hit the cabin wall and tumbled to the floor. Everything went black. When he opened his eyes, the floor carpet was inches from his nose. Disorientated, he looked around the cabin. Everything spun. He closed his eyes, aware of the shooting pain in his neck that continued down his left arm. He tried to sit up, but his arm wouldn't obey. It left a bitter taste in his mouth. The pin had broken away, sliced through his nerves; just what he'd been told would happen if he didn't take care. Yet another reason to retire. *Andromeda* was cursed, and now his arm was paralyzed.

The scramjet continued to shake. It lurched left and then right.

Leece appeared next to him. "Are you all right?"

He focused, tried to still the spinning, and nodded. The scramjet's flight path didn't seem right.

"Help me up. I need to get to the flight cabin."

Autopilot could be ineffective. Hot pockets of air were playing havoc with the AI. It wasn't human. It didn't comprehend.

He raised his right arm. Leece helped him up and onto the empty flight deck. He strapped himself into the pilot's chair and took the controls.

He had been too long away from the pilot's seat.

Leece took the seat beside him and strapped herself in. "What are you going to do?"

"The AI can't cope. We will have to do it ourselves."

"Fly it?" Her hands went to her mouth. "When did you become a pilot?"

"Technically, I didn't. I'm an ex... astronaut... deep-space trained. This was my ship, *Andromeda*, before they did the mods for Earth flights. I know everything about her." He touched the instrumentation panel.

"You've never mentioned this before?"

He closed his eyes and swallowed. When he opened them again, his voice caught. "I don't enjoy talking about my failures. If she wasn't sound, I reckon we'd have found out already." He leaned in and looked at her. "We don't want that, do we?"

"No." She shook her head. Color seeped back into her face.

He looked at the projected images — their 'window' outside — down at the chaotic sea of molten lava below. How could so much of the Earth be covered? Volcanic ash reduced their visibility, and he wondered how long it would be before ash ruined the cameras. His eyes danced over the gauges. They seemed fine.

His left arm hung lifeless as he took a breath. He disengaged the AI. Using his right hand, he pulled back on the controls and felt her climb out of the jets of lava. The South Pole wouldn't be hard to find, and he could switch on the AI when they arrived. He wasn't ready to attempt a landing.

ALAN HOPED THAT THE knot in his stomach would relinquish its grip as the South Pole and Mawson City loomed closer. But molten lava covered the land. Nothing remained and there was no sign of standing buildings or life.

"How? Why?" said Leece.

He shook his head. "I have no idea..."

"Where do we go now?"

Looking at the sea of molten lava, Alan was beyond words. The Poles had been humanity's last stand.

"Why?"

Again he had no answer. The knot in his stomach tightened to match the lump in his throat.

"What now?" Leece's tears fell unhindered.

"There's the Drake Outpost—" he forced out.

"The moon?"

He nodded. "As a last resort, but I don't think I'm capable of flying *Andromeda* there. There has to be somewhere else—"

"What about Europa Base?"

"Of course." He nodded. Why didn't he think of that? He squeezed her hand. "We can only hope."

Alan adjusted *Andromeda's* flight path and pushed the old girl up and away from the crippling images of what had been Mawson City. Leece sat next to him, but she was moving into shock. He needed to talk to her, keep her mind on other things, but what could he say? He couldn't think of anything, and he had to keep the scramjet up and out of the hot jets of air and lava. Above, a blanket of thick ash closed in. He had no idea what to do if Europa wasn't there. They climbed into sub-orbital space for a horrific view of a world on fire. As they flew into the night, a sea of molten red glowed angrily below them, but it grew cold in the cabin. He grabbed a blanket and put it over Leece's shoulders, but she didn't register or shift her glazed stare.

AT THE EQUATOR, ALAN sat up and felt his first glimmer of relief. "Well, I'll be darned. Leece, look." He switched the AI back on and set it to land.

She turned to him. "How?"

"I don't know." His neck ached, and his arm still wouldn't respond, but the knot in his stomach loosened. He had no idea how the sea and this part of the world had been left untouched by volcanic activity.

As they stepped out of the scramjet, Alan was shocked to find everything exactly as they had left it.

"Where are the guards?" asked Leece when nobody met them.

"I don't know."

"So what do we do now?"

"For the moment, take stock of rations and equipment. I will spend the afternoon stripping *Andromeda*. Then I reckon we should get some rest."

"So we're not flying to the moon?"

He shook his head and looked at the scramjet. "I wouldn't trust her to remain airtight in space."

ALAN WOKE AT THE BANGING on the door of the hut and a man calling out. "Dr. Derringer." It was ten in the morning, and he smiled at Leece, next to him in the bed.

She smiled back. "You should answer that. I think our honeymoon is over." She raised her left hand and stared at the ring.

"Just a minute," he yelled through the door.

"Roger that."

As nice as their night had been, it had been a wild, passionate moment, where they had pushed reality away for a few hours, for a night. Together, they stepped out into a sun-filled vista. Here, what had happened yesterday at Meridian and Mawson City seemed remote.

It surprised Alan to see a dozen poorly dressed men and women with Geoff. They looked back at Alan with suspicion.

Geoff stepped forward, away from the group. "Dr. Moran." He smiled at Leece, gesturing to the sling. "Have an accident, Dr. Derringer?"

"Yes, during the flight out of Meridian City." Alan's voice caught in his throat.

"Is it true? You saw it for yourself?"

Alan closed his eyes. Emotion welled up inside of him. He felt Leece grab his hand and squeeze it tight. He took a deep breath, barely able to speak. "Yes, both cities were completely destroyed. I'm sorry."

Through a firestorm of emotions, the man still said, "How?"

Alan shook his head. He had nothing to add.

"So, we're all that's left?"

"It is possible there are pockets of people," said Alan, showing the group behind Geoff.

Geoff cleared his throat. "Yep, these are wonderful people. When we heard the news of what was happening, we went to see about getting their help. We gave them our medical supplies, and they've promised to speak to their leaders and their military for us. We should be safe enough, but I admit it is risky."

"So you will join them?"

"Yep. They're living in a cave by the sea. The water and conditions are far better than we had believed."

"Better how?"

Geoff shrugged. "Come with us, sir, and find out. I'm sure that with your expertise you'll be welcomed."

Alan looked at Leece. "Well?"

She nodded. "I want to discover why this region has been unaffected by the chaos."

Geoff stepped forward. "Perhaps it's the bacteria?"

Alan frowned. "I don't see how. Bacteria don't quell volcanic activity."

"Perhaps Mother Earth, Gaia, is telling us something?"

"No, the scientist in me can't buy that either."

"What then?"

Alan sighed. "Honestly, I have no idea."

"Then stay here, sir, take more measurements, find out what's going on. Research the bacteria and this region."

Leece stepped forward and put her hand on his arm. "What alternatives do we have, Alan?"

Alan turned and looked at *Andromeda*.

"You should launch her into space, sir, as a tribute to the fallen," said Geoff. "God knows what we will do with her otherwise."

Emotion churned within him, and the memories of *Centaurus* and her launch grew. What use was *Andromeda* now to anyone here?

"What about it, Dr. Derringer?"

Alan looked at them, aware that all eyes were on him.

THE TRIP TO THE SETTLEMENT was more than a journey. For Alan and Leece it was the start of a fresh life, and they had no doubts as to the coming hardships.

It had felt right to launch *Andromeda*, to allow her to begin her journey into deep space. It was a fitting tribute to the people of Mawson City and of Meridian City, who had perished, and to the crew of *Centaurus*.

Pulling out the mission data from *Andromeda's* navigation computer and punching in the same mission coordinates as the original Cassini Probe had been an act of blind faith; to send her out into the far reaches of the universe for another civilization.

He had to believe that there was some truth to the signals received by the Drake Outpost on the moon; but they'd never really know. Putting the bacteria samples aboard felt right, too, a gift to the cosmos. Perhaps *Andromeda* would find other life.

No matter what else happened to Earth, the bacteria tucked away in *Andromeda's* hold could one day become Gaia's legacy.

GAIA'S LANDFALL

Myra saw death in the discolored coral and in the warmer sea currents that spread pollutants over their communal pod-homes. She blamed the dry-lands high above them. Light penetrated the depths to where smaller schools of fish that once avoided the colder regions now descended. They hid in the warmer pockets near her pod-house.

When reports that an off-world craft had landed up on the dry-lands, the Administrators — so tied up with their governing bureaucracy and their own self-importance — announced that the distant Terrans had arrived.

Myra had scoffed. How could the Administrators know it was from Terra? But there was a lot she didn't know, and as a youngling fresh out of university she needed to find out more. Oceania and the Goddess Anthe demanded it.

Myra, Somni, and Rhu, swam upwards into the forbidden layers. Myra drew mouthfuls of nourishing liquid ethane into her lungs, sure that the other two younglings who followed also mentally prepared themselves to beach. Each stroke, every kick, took them further from the comforts of their communal pod-homes and closer to the forbidden, unknown dry-lands, to the off-world craft that was the source of the radio signal. To Landfall.

Myra hid her doubts. She dared not admit she was out of her depth. She had never been so high before, but there wasn't time to stop and admire the industrial landmarks as they ascended. They had six cycles of their moon, Kria, barely a third of a day before the stubborn

Administrators unleashed their plasma bomb and destroyed the off-world craft.

At any other time, Myra would have embraced the opportunity to explore the remote tungsten mines. As they passed, she could feel the shock waves from the tungsten powder metallurgy site. Workers used under-ethane explosive compaction techniques to create metal that would end up as micron-thick parts for industry.

She swam upwards, fought the drag of the Exoskeleton Load Carrier hooked behind her, and cursed the weight of its bulky telluric batteries. She was sure that the other two also struggled, but she refused to turn and look back at them, it would be a sign a weakness and she couldn't allow herself any room for doubt right now. Weighty as they were, they would each need an ELC if they were to survive the dry-lands.

"Breather helmets on," she advised, more than a little afraid, and pulled her visor down to protect her eyes from the harsh above-world light. She tugged on the fine chain that connected her to Somni and Rhu and stirred them into action.

"Yes, Myra," they replied dutifully in unison.

Landfall approached and as Myra stared up into the bright light, imaginary Crayfish twisted and turned in her stomach.

MYRA WAITED WITH SOMNI at Landfall, the edge of the world, and they watched the slower Rhu join them.

"Ready?" asked Myra when Rhu arrived and puffed loudly.

Myra checked her chronometer when they each nodded. "We have two cycles to get there, a cycle to explore and then two to get back. That leaves us a cycle spare, just in case, and then the Administrators launch their Plasma bomb. I'll go first like we planned."

"Good luck." Rhu squeezed her hand.

"Be careful," added Somni.

Myra put on a brave face and smiled at them. She stared into the harsh light of Landfall above, the cornerstone of their world. From here on in they risked everything and if they weren't careful, would join a list of other explorers who'd never returned. She prayed to the Goddess that their pressurized tanks and the Exoskeleton Load Carriers would work.

Myra pulled up her fat-lined suit. They made it from the skin of a rhino-fish, and she hoped it would protect her from the harsh above-world environment.

Myra's hand shook as turned her ethane supply on and clambered upwards out of the protective sea, and onto the harsh dry-lands at Landfall.

MYRA BELIEVED IN THE legend of Anthe, the mother Goddess of Oceania, who gave her son a sickle before he killed his father with it. The blood drops that fell spawned a universe of her children in the form of rich new worlds. Before Anthe died, she promised to visit, and to gift them eternal life.

That was why the off-world craft had arrived. It was the Goddess Anthe's gift to save Oceania. Why else would it arrive when they were most in need?

Myra shuddered at the sight of the dense atmosphere, so unlike their ocean. It was horrid. Thick opaque clouds rained down poisonous liquid. The moisture turned into a thick warm mist at ground level.

She stepped onto her Exoskeleton Load Carrier and waited for the others to climb onto their own. The ELC machine would do the walking for each of them, protect their webs from the harsh ground, and carry their supplies.

Myra faced Somni. "Tell me you used the telluric currents to charge the Load Carrier's batteries?"

"Yes, Myra. The ELC's batteries are charged." Somni's voice sounded distinct through the helmet's earphones.

"They can't fail us," she urged.

"We're tough enough to traverse the dry-lands," said Somni.

"We're not, Somni. Look at this place." Rhu pulled out her monitor from its pouch. "This atmosphere is unbreathable."

"What does it say?" Somni leaned toward the monitor.

"We're bathing in a soup of nitrogen, hydrocarbons, carbon dioxide, ethane rain, and corrosive hydrogen cyanide."

Somni waved her helmet with a gloved hand. "You might be right. It's already so hot up here! And you say this isn't crazy, Myra?" Somni shook her head.

Myra wondered how to reply. Even with the visor's filter, she squinted against the bright light. "We can do it." But now they were here, she wasn't as convinced.

"Swordfish!" Rhu cried out as she slipped from her ELC and fell onto the rocky ground.

"Careful, Rhu. Are you right?" Somni stepped from her ELC.

"I'm fine. Stay there." Rhu stood and dusted herself off. "Look," she pointed to the large ringed object that appeared through a break in the thick clouds. "It's Kria."

Myra grinned as she stared up at the moon. With no viewing equipment, it was breathtaking. At any other time, she might have stared at it forever, but not now. Today they had to get to the off-world craft.

Myra took in the two youngling females with a glance one last time and wondered what three younglings from different pods could do. Rhu had bigger bones than she and Somni. But then Rhu's pod was typical of a pale-skinned, red-haired clan, and she had the lightest blue eyes Myra had ever seen. Somni was small, dark-skinned, with tough black hair, and seemed far more resilient. Against them, Myra felt insignificant with her green-blonde hair and olive complexion. Green eyes were so plain. She wished she were more like Somni; resilience would help them on the dry-lands.

"Come on," she said and stepped forward. Apprehension filled her. Her breathing apparatus straps were too tight. It was far too hot at the surface, and their equipment weighed her down. She glanced back and threw them a last smile. She had no doubts that dry-land travel would be very difficult and they may never return.

"Let's go," she said with a hard lump in her throat and engaged her ELC drives.

THREE CYCLES OF THE moon Kria passed and every step of the ELC wore away at Myra's resolve. The ELC was harder to use than she'd imagined. Three cycles remained, and already they had chewed up their spare cycle of time before they had arrived. Doubt clawed at her over their chances to return to Landfall.

When Rhu's forced breaths echoed in Myra's headset, she didn't have the heart to tell the youngling girl that her microphone was set to voice activate. Perhaps Rhu knew, and she wanted to broadcast her concern.

The heat seared, sunlight burned with a vengeance that she had not expected. Myra felt it through the thick layer of fat beneath her suit.

Looking around at the landscape, nothing grew; there was no coral in sight, no fish, and no crustaceans. The dry-lands were devoid of life.

In the distance, a slight hill stood out against an otherwise flat ground. Perhaps when they reached it the view would change.

"How much further?" Somni's voice sounded metallic and strained through the helmet transducers.

"Not long." Myra closed her eyes and hoped that it was the case.

"We've run out of time." Panic rose in Rhu's reply.

Myra took a slow deep breath and fought what was probably a similar urge to run away. "We'll just have to make up for time somehow."

But Rhu was right; they had run out of time before they had reached the site of the alien radio transmissions. "How are everyone's tanks?"

"Mine's just over half full," said Somni.

"Mine's well past half empty," said Rhu.

Myra and Somni stopped and faced each other. Somni's furrowed brow turned into a frown. Rhu had slowed them up for most of the trek, and she had used more from her tank than Myra and Rhu. It shouldn't have been the case.

"Perhaps you should turn back, Rhu?" said Somni. It made sense and Myra nodded.

"I'm not going back after coming this far. You said it yourself, we're almost there."

Myra sighed. "try to save your fluids. Breath slower if you can." She wondered if Rhu would make it back with them. If any of them made it back at all.

"But it's worse than I could have imagined. How can it be so hot and cloudy?" asked Rhu.

No wonder no one had ever returned from the dry-lands. But Myra kept her thoughts to herself. "Don't talk, Rhu. Conserve your energy."

"What's the point?" said Rhu. "I'll be out of fluid before I can return. I will die out here. I can feel it, and it's—"

"Nonsense." Somni's voice cut like a knife.

It was unlike her, but it was what Rhu needed, and the youngling went quiet. "Come here, Rhu," said Myra. "Let me see your tank."

"Her tank is leaking," said Somni as she climbed off the ELC.

"What?" Rhu spun in a circle and fell from her ELC to her knees. She cut herself on the rocky ground and cried out.

Somni scrambled over to Rhu with all the finesse of a jellyfish climbing the coral reefs.

"Careful of the rocks, Rhu," Myra warned, and she could have hit herself. "How can it leak?" Her shoulders sagged as she climbed down and joined the others. It had been her responsibility, but she *had* checked everything before they left. She tightened the pressure relief valve and watched the leak dissipate. Myra cursed. Why hadn't she thought to check for leaks sooner?

Somni stepped forward. "It must have been damaged when Rhu fell at Landfall."

Myra closed her eyes. What hadn't she thought to check the girl's tank? "Somni, check my tank."

"It's fine," Somni said moments later. "How's mine?"

"Yours is good," she said.

"Don't worry, Rhu, we'll rebalance our tanks so we all have the same amount when we get there." Somni smiled, but her concern was obvious though the helmet.

A death wish, that's what it was. And it was Myra's fault. She should have left Rhu when they beached at Landfall. She didn't share the belief in the Goddess like Somni. But it was too late now. They were all in this together.

Myra cringed at the large round disk in the sky, to the sun that sapped their strength. It wasn't any wonder they lived far below the dry-lands.

HARD, POROUS ROCK GAVE way to fine sand that would have burned even more than the rocks without the ELCs. Myra stopped and applied a salve of codfish oil over her suit and then climbed the hill. She encouraged plump Rhu forward, but her heart caught each time she noticed the dwindling level of the youngling's tank supply.

Ever positive, Somni smiled back at Myra and pressed on.

She loved her for that.

Rhu stopped ahead of them at the top of the hill and pointed. "There it is."

Myra increased her pace.

"And there is a small sea." Rhu yelled and then disappeared over the hilltop.

"Rhu, wait!" Myra forced herself up the hill as fast as the ELC's batteries could cope with.

Rhu took no notice of her or the hot sandy ground. She clambered from the ELC and made her way across the flat open land. She approached the enormous sea, careless of the off-world craft that was half buried below the surface.

Myra stood in awe of the craft. It glistened.

Somni arrived as Rhu dropped to her knees near the edge of the smaller sea.

Myra pressed her intercom control. "Rhu, don't!"

"I'm thirsty." Rhu's words were sprinkled with joy in Myra's earpieces.

Somni's voice boomed through their headsets, full of concern. "What are you doing, Rhu? It might be poisonous."

But Rhu hadn't heard, or she ignored the warning, and pulled off her helmet and lowered her head below the surface.

Somni pushed her ELC down the hill toward Rhu. Myra unclipped her heavy pack and followed carefully on foot.

Somni reached Rhu first and pulled her up out of the sea. Together, Myra and Somni put Rhu's helmet back on and sat her down on the sandy shore.

Rhu laughed. "It's gassy, like Sparks."

Somni stood in front of Rhu, hands on her hips. "You're crazy. What were you thinking?"

"You saw my tank supplies."

"You should have waited until they tested it," said Myra.

"Always the scientist, Myra. Trust me, it's fine."

Myra sat down and sighed. Rhu looked fine, at least for now.

"Let's see." Somni pulled the monitor from its pouch and placed the probe into the liquid.

Myra hoped for good news.

They waited until the results appeared on the display.

"What is it?" Myra leaned in.

"Give me a moment," said Somni.

"Ethane?" asked Rhu.

Somni nodded. "And methane. Dissolved carbon dioxide—"

"Yes," said Rhu.

"That's weird. And free oxygen in the form of di-oxygen, and a variant with hydrogen."

"Free oxygen?" Myra frowned. "Are you sure?"

She nodded. "It's a first."

"Sparks plus then." Rhu laughed.

"So," asked Myra. "Is it safe enough to drink?"

"I guess," said Somni.

Rhu laughed. "Told you so."

Myra stood, she stole a glance at the off-world craft and a shudder of excitement ran through her. Perhaps with this sea, they had bought some time, even if it wouldn't stop the Plasma bomb. She glanced at her chronometer. "There's two-and-a-half cycles before the bomb destroys this site. I'll collect some of this fluid in case we need it, then equalize our tanks. Somni, you and Rhu check out the off-world craft, and Somni, monitor Rhu, in case she has a turn."

"Done," said Somni.

"I'll be fine, Myra," said Rhu. "Your Goddess Anthe will take care of us." Rhu giggled.

Myra half-dismissed the comment but couldn't be sure if there was an element of belief from Rhu. Being up here would change anyone. She sat for a moment and calculated their time. It had taken them three and a half cycles to get here, and if she allowed a quarter to explore, then the two and a quarter cycles that remained to travel back would leave them short by a cycle. Even if they could use some liquid ethane from the small sea, they couldn't avoid being caught at the edge of the plasma bomb blast when it went off. She sighed, past trying to show enthusiasm. "Be quick, everyone. We're here for a quarter of Kyria's cycle and then we have to go!"

MYRA COULDN'T HELP but get drawn by the off-world craft. It half-sat in the sea, taller than them all, a grey unfamiliar object that cut a harsh angular shape.

She stood at the base. "Somni, what have you discovered?"

"It's metallic, of a sort I have never seen. And Rhu has found some etched symbols on the side." Somni pointed. "Look."

"I will. Excellent work, Rhu."

Myra stepped closer to the structure, full of sharp angles, and wondered where it had come from. The design had none of the rounded, soft curves of their world.

Somni stepped closer with the scanner device.

"What do you think it is?" asked Myra.

"Not sure."

"You're the expert. See any molecular self-assembly protocols?"

"No." Somni shook her head. "I'd guess it's inanimate."

Myra leaned toward it. "What is it doing?"

Somni faced her. "Lots! It's transmitting, collecting intelligence, and analyzing us."

"Do you think its information processing dominates its structure?" Myra realized that Som would scoff at her textbook question.

But she didn't. "Wow! You're suggesting this is artificial life!"

Myra shrugged. "Perhaps." She placed her hand to touch it, but stopped short. What if it was alive and waited for just that?

"I'm still scanning but the initial readings show it's a non-living system. There's no armament, and it doesn't appear to be a threat, at least to us."

"What's inside then?"

"It is full of sensors, but shows no obvious spontaneity regarding its information processing."

"So it's *not* alive?"

"No biological life either, it's just scanning, and transmitting the results."

"Have you recorded all that?"

Somni nodded. "Rhu already did, I'm just rechecking."

"If it's not an AI, or self-assembled, then a life-form still sent it," said Myra.

"But from where?"

"You heard the Administrators," said Myra. "Terra, wherever that is."

"How do they know that?"

"You know better than ask, Somni." Myra shrugged. "All I found out was that we have been monitoring Terran abnormal emissions for centuries. Younglings aren't advanced enough to be trusted with any other information."

"I disagree," said Somni.

"Well, we all do, otherwise we wouldn't be here but that doesn't change their view."

"I know. I just think it's wrong." Somni moved around to the back of the craft. "Come look at the plate Rhu found. It has pictures on it." She laughed. "It's of a man and a woman."

Myra joined her and laughed too. "What a strange race of beings. Take a copy."

"They aren't so unlike us. Just look at their short legs."

Myra smiled. "They're fat, with small narrow eyes."

Somni laughed. "I wonder if they are like us, I mean *really* like us."

"You heard the Administrators," said Myra. "They translated an encrypted signal from Landfall via the photonics feed. They have to be just like us—" Myra paused as the alarm went off in her headset. "Everyone get that?"

"Yes," said Somni.

"Rhu?"

"Yes, Myra, time to go before we get blown to pieces."

"Finished copying the symbols, Somni?"

"Yes." Somni put the recorder away in her pack.

"I still can't understand why the Administrators want to destroy it," said Somni.

"Because they're smart," said Rhu. "The ancestors genetically modified us, and then turned their back on us. We need to destroy—"

"Stories Rhu," said Somni. "We're not mutated Terrans."

"You're wrong. We came from Terra, and they've never been back until now. They're a threat."

"That's ridiculous. Where's your proof, Rhu?"

Rhu pointed to the craft. "There's my proof."

"But it proves nothing except there is life out there. We should cherish that, not destroy it."

"It doesn't prove they're here to help, Somni. If they are here, then they want something. They have no rights and the Administrators are right in neutralizing any threats to Oceania."

"Where is the threat, Rhu? Oceania has always been our world, nobody else's." Somni stood proudly. "All it proves is that the legend of the Goddess Anthe is real."

"All right, enough." Myra wanted to believe that there was a reason for the craft being here. Perhaps the legend was right. Perhaps the Goddess Anthe was Terran. The legend had said that Anthe promised to visit and gift them eternal life. But who could say? "I don't think the Administrators should destroy it, but if we stand here, we won't find out anything about the Goddess Anthe, or Terra, or an alien race that might threaten us. The Administrators will destroy this area, no matter what we think or do."

"The Administrators probably don't even know we've gone."

Myra nodded, but in her heart she knew that sensors would have tracked their journey with interest. The unanswered question was if any of the youngling boys she had spoken to before they had left could do anything to delay the bomb?

"Myra, there's something there too," said Rhu.

Somni laughed as Rhu pointed to the small sea. "You mean like a Conja?"

Myra smiled, "It's too shallow to hide a giant, razor-toothed eel, don't you think?"

"No." Rhu ignored them. "I saw a cloud of material moving just below the surface."

"Moving you say?" Myra turned to stare at the sea's still surface.

"You're the microbiologist, look." Rhu laughed. "And breath in the bubbles of gas, it's amazing. Better than Sparks."

"That's what you breathed in? Something alive?" asked Myra.

"You should have said. You should know better," said Somni.

Rhu shrugged under Myra's fiery glare. "We should take some back with us. It will die with the bomb."

"We can't. There's no time." Somni's expression was adamant.

"It's life, Somni. It's sacred." Rhu turned to Myra. "What if this is the Goddess' gift? You must!"

"I didn't think you believed in the Goddess, Rhu?" asked Myra.

She shrugged. "I didn't but look at this place. It's even bigger than our sea-world. And I can see the heavens when the clouds shift. It's beautiful."

Myra nodded. Rhu made sense. Perhaps the Goddess Anthe's gift of eternal life was not the off-word craft but a life form that had stowed aboard? Something to save Oceania.

"I'll get a container," she said. But Somni was right, too. They had run out of time. Perhaps the Goddess would intervene and allow them more time.

MYRA FORCED HER HEAD and shoulders into the murky-brown sea. It wasn't like she imagined. It was warm enough to be fed from a hot thermal vent deep within Oceania. She focused on the steady stream of cloudy material below and wondered if the bacterial life was a product of the corrosive hydrogen cyanide. It had to have come from somewhere.

The turbid mass moved away from her hand, sluggish, as if it struggled at existence. Perhaps it would die out here under these desolate conditions? She doubted it would survive the Plasma bomb.

She raised her arm behind her back and signaled for a container. As a microbiologist, she knew better than to take her eyes from a sample before they had collected it. Myra felt the container in her hand, and then she pushed it down and scooped up the cloudy matter. She raised her hand again, this time with the sample in it, and when it was replaced with an empty container, she filled that one too. She contemplated removing her mask and breathe in the liquid, but refrained. Instead, she thrust the monitor close to the source of hot liquid, and wasn't surprised that it showed high levels of methane, carbon dioxide and an abundance of free oxygen. It had to be the bacteria.

She stood and walked out of the lake. "It's unlike anything I've ever seen. It has to be responsible for the free oxygen."

"We're late," said Somni.

Myra read her chronometer and scowled. They had less than two cycles.

"Everyone ready?"

"Good," she said when they both nodded. "Let's go."

THEY PUSHED THE ELCS as fast as they would go, careless to everything, and only concerned with trying to purchase as much distance as they could from the bomb.

They ran in the ELCs. And ran. Pushed themselves to their limits.

"My tank's empty," said Rhu.

There was panic in Rhu's voice through the headset. Myra checked her own gauge, and the imaginary Crayfish returned to the pit of her stomach as she discovered her tank was almost empty.

She unslung the container of contaminated liquid from the above-world sea and handed it to Rhu to breathe from. Then they took it in turns to recharge their tanks.

"We have to go," cried Somni.

Myra nodded. Too filled with concern to speak, she pressed on again.

The ELCs slowed as the batteries drained of their charge. Myra all but held her breath, as they ventured into a thick fog-infested landscape so devoid of life she never wanted to return. Acid dripped off the titanium ELC housings and Somni's battery failed.

Myra wasn't surprised.

If there had been somewhere close to replace the metal plates and repair the telluric battery, they still wouldn't have had time. Forget that they needed to be closer to their world's core to recharge the battery.

Myra frowned as she read her chronometer, sick to her stomach. They were light on fluids and had half a cycle before the bomb went off. They wouldn't survive the plasma blast at that rate.

"Somni, climb on to mine. Essential items only," said Myra.

When Somni was settled, they set off again.

Myra pushed the two ELC's forward toward the safety of Landfall, harder and faster than she had before. It didn't matter that they broke as long as it was outside the blast zone.

Relentless, they pushed on and Rhu led the way on her lighter ELC. She disappeared from sight as she climbed over the crest of a hill. Myra's ELC slowed and then stopped.

Myra pressed her intercom. "Rhu can you hear me?"

There was no reply.

Myra faced Somni as the imaginary Crayfish returned in greater numbers and twisted and turned in her stomach until she wanted to throw up. "The battery is dead."

"What do we do now?" asked Somni.

"Help me unpack. Grab what you can carry."

Somni agree and together they removed the bacteria and other essential items.

Before they had finished, Somni stood and pointed as Rhu returned on her ELC. She circled them and stepped from her ELC.

"What happened?" asked Rhu.

"No time. Battery's dead. Here take these." Myra handed Rhu the bacteria samples, the data they had collected, and some of their fluid supplies.

"Go!" said Somni. "We'll catch up with you at Landfall."

"I can't," said Rhu. "It's not right to leave you."

"There's room for one of you. Myra? Somni?"

Myra faced Somni.

"No." Somni shook her head. "We can't risk overloading her battery."

Rhu stepped forward. "Somni, you're the lightest of us all. You must go in my place. You stand the best chance."

"No!" Somni shook her head vigorously.

"Rhu's right, Somni. You know it," said Myra. She smiled at Rhu, proudly.

Myra stepped forward and hugged Somni. "You are the Goddess' sickle now. Run for us. Build a new world with her gift in the hot ocean vents," said Myra.

"Do what she says, Somni." Rhu stumbled over and hugged Somni.

"Thank you. But hurry after me." Tears fell down her face as she stowed her load.

"We will," said Myra. They watched Somni speed away on the ELC.

Myra faced Rhu. "Run. Whatever you do, don't stop, and don't look back."

Rhu threw Myra a half smile and together they ran, side by side.

MYRA'S SIDE HURT FROM running. Razor sharp stones sliced through her rhino-fish suit and cut deep into her webs. With every step she couldn't help but cry out in pain.

Rhu's discomfort was just as loud in Myra's headset. She glanced at her chronometer and bit her lip until she could taste blood. All she could do now was hope that the youngling boys had stopped or delayed the bomb going off. "Say a prayer to the Goddess, Rhu, and just keep running." She turned off the link between them before Rhu could reply and pushed on as best as she could.

When the atmosphere lit up in a kaleidoscope of bright and painful colour Myra had no regrets.

As it threw her onto the hard dry ground, hot plasma-fire tore at her back. It burned away her protective suit and ignited the fat layer. The off-world craft would have been destroyed, the sea, contaminated from an off-world bacteria, would have gone. She closed her eyes, unable to fight the pain that took her, and said a silent prayer hoping the Goddess Anthe allowed her sickle, Somni, to have survived the Plasma bomb and bring new life to Oceania.

And then darkness took her, and nothing...

PART II: HALACONIA

HALACONIA'S VIRUS

I am Gaia's sister, and my name is Halaconia.

Frozen beyond belief, I travelled, lost and isolated, until I found this region. It drew me in: a fresh new galaxy so like mine before it went supernova.

I was part of an edge world before they launched me into the void. Until I found the sweet seductive pull of Sol. I collided with Gaia — my new sister — and out of the entanglement we were both reformed. She with much of me, and I with some of her: mainly her outer skin. I think Gaia won from the merging because the life within me spawned on Gaia — and failed — while hers thrived like a virus that would not let up.

I can only hope that my seed has found a niche on the remnants of myself: something now referred to as The Moon, but I will always consider myself Halaconia, proud with a history I ache to tell. I had believed that perhaps my offspring — that life which I hold dear — would eventually take hold and prove its worth in this region. I was convinced we could coexist as equals.

I had thought even if my seed had to lie dormant for an eternity — until I could finally welcome them — perhaps then as Gaia's Children, you might of sensed a kindred spirit as it emerged.

But that wasn't to be — I got my wish: my siblings have been freed — and here are some snippets as the children of both sisters met.

CHIP'S STORY: SPRINKLE ME WITH MOON DUST GOLD

I think we are driven by two goals in life: one is to be successful and judge ourselves by the shine in another person's eye, and the other is to find the love a beautiful person, genuine love that tempts you to do anything. I achieved — and lost — both on the moon.

I left Earth with a vision of being independent, of living my life separate — like a Spaniard explorer in the New World — but the moon had much less to offer, and I remained dependent on Earth, even if I, and everyone else in the colony, wanted to think otherwise.

I'd caught the Mooltan shuttle over in the rush of 2064, and like most of the passengers, boasted I'd become so rich I'd be able to return home and buy a European state.

I sunk most of my savings into a Command Mining Unit. The CMU all terrain tracked mobile vehicle had gold mining sluices and a mineral extraction unit. I'd painted my name, Chip, on the side so people knew me. The rest of my savings had gone on a year's accommodation in the small Carson City Dome on the south of the Sea of Tranquility, and on barely enough food, air and water.

Imagine the wonders, the riches in a million years of asteroid dust just lying in wait: craters full of gold, rare earth metals, minerals; including elements that we'd haven't even discovered yet.

I mined the crater dust out on the Sea of Tranquility. I worked long and hard. I slowly accumulated significant wealth: gold, titanium, and rare space elements my CMU cataloged and stored. I sold my mine tailings — remnants of million-year-old moon dust — to the Lunar Climate Change Company. They needed tons of dust grains every year and took everything I offered and seeded an enormous cloud about 4000 kilometers in radius out in the first Earth-Sun Lagrange position. They said they had reduced the effects of climate change. I didn't care so much: it was hot on the moon when we were in sunlight and freezing when it went dark, but I got accustomed to the long fourteen-day cycle of day and night. Most of us kept Earth-time. However, it was just easier that way.

After work, I'd sit and have a drink and listen to the stories that the dome-building workers bragged about as they constructed the super dome over Tranquility where I worked emptying the crater. They weren't as tough as they made out and just wanted be entertained at the end of a busy day.

It was there, I'd met Clara Belle, and looking across the smoky-filled bar, I reckoned she could only have been seventeen, sitting there with her stepsister Mary-Lou. They travelled in the company of an older man, Percy, a philosopher — and one of the European Lords whose name I never heard mentioned because he had got Mary-Lou pregnant out on the trip to the moon. They were all here to write of adventure, create poems and dream of a new world. They'd come to the right place.

I fell for Clara Belle on sight. I'd like to think we fell for each other: that there was a chemistry that drew us together. But for a time we were inseparable, and when we weren't in my private quarters, I'd listen to her and her companions write poetry about the moon and each other and discuss what sort of world the new moon colony would be.

One day in my room, she said to sprinkle her with moon dust gold. Who wouldn't want to cover her in asteroid and meteorite gold that had lain dormant for so many millions of years? She was beautiful before I did, but exquisite after the fact. Her pale skin shimmered in the earthlight. Soon after, she left when her troupe of bohemian companions caught a return shuttle to Earth. It devastated me for a time.

They say that a fool and his money are easily parted, but I'd like to think I'd paid a fair price for the experience. Nobody can take those memories of that time from me, and after all I understand that we are nothing but a collection of memories, and it's what you do with them that defines you. I'd seen the shine in another man's eye when I'd been seen with her, even experienced the love a beautiful woman: I know when I'm done mining she'll be waiting for me on Earth like she promised.

THE DOME OVER TRANQUILITY is all but finished. My CMU has run out of mining dust. There is an opportunity to move on to Serenity, follow the dome builders and sell more of my tailings to keep Earth's climate in check. But I'm after bigger fish, I think I've grown tired of this experience, and I've more than covered the gold I lost that day Clara Belle glistened with love. I've heard there's a team heading north to the pole: ice miners, cutting fresh water to fill the Sea of Tranquility. That's where I'm going. After all, there is a lifetime of opportunities here and I've plenty of moon dust gold.

GRANTHAM'S STORY: THE MOON'S SOUL

I never really understood what drove me to the moon. Perhaps it was the apocalypse and watching the gradual death of the world's oceans: everyone said Grantham Millar was a fool for immigrating to the Moon's colony. I didn't: I found you could take chemical warfare one step too far. Perhaps it was a sense of adventure and an opportunity for a new life. For me, the Moon and the Earth were oceans apart: well, they were by the time we'd finished mining ice from the Moon's poles.

I told my son, and my young grandson, that the *Sea of Tranquility* is neither a veritable sea nor a tranquil place, although we tried to make it both. Nowadays, I'm too old to care. We'd dreamed of creating a world in the image of Earth before much of the oceans fouled. I was on the moon from the beginning: with men like me — ice miners who toiled at the moon's poles — we watched the domes go up over the *Sea of Tranquility*, and *Serenity*.

I kicked a rock into *Tranquility's* water's edge and watched the ripples form. I sat in my deck chair, careful not to spill my ice-moon wine: sweet wine timed to mature on the vine during the last two weeks of the season when night fell. Mary-Lou had passed a few years back, and it reminded me of our holidays in the south of France. I raised my glass to her beautiful memory and toasted our life together. It wasn't long after that the poison spread across Earth's oceans, and now I appreciated the Moon's oceans had more fish and the people fewer, so I'd like to think we were better off; but I'm not convinced. There's *something* about this place that isn't right, something I can't put my finger on.

It wasn't always like this. When I arrived on the moon, *Tranquility* was a bowl of dust. I remember they had a crew moving as much of the crater dust over to the vineyard and vegetable plots as they could. I closed my eyes, time fell away, and I recalled my aching arm...

"Ouch!" I rubbed my upper arm. "What are the inoculations really for?" I said.

The nurse with the expressionless face shrugged. "Encephalitis."

"How are we going to catch encephalitis on the moon?" I asked. "There's nobody there!"

"Just take the shot! We'll all be there," said another ice-miner.

"The company has strict policies," she said. "Nobody goes to the moon without *all* the mandatory shots. That way nobody can catch anything from anyone else."

"Okay," I shrugged. "Give me the rest of them." It seemed like an excellent idea.

"Can't stop the flu," said an ice miner. "It'll morph soon enough and we'll all have moon flu."

The men standing in line behind me laughed. "Man flu."

"From all the cheese culture," said another miner.

I smiled over the memories. We'd laughed a lot, and mostly all got on well, considering where we were and the hardships' we'd endured. For the most of us it was tough work — cutting enormous chunks of fresh ice from the frozen poles. Lunar Enterprises lured us with a false promise of two weeks on and two weeks off. We'll fly you to the other side of the Moon, they said, so you can enjoy endless sunshine. What I didn't appreciate was that in some crevices on the poles, it was always dark, and the ice-cutting suits were never thick enough to keep out the biting cold. I never lost a finger, or any of my toes, or anything else, but I worked near the surface, and Mary-Lou stayed loyal to me. She put up with the isolation for the eight years we mined the ice, trucked it across the surface to *Tranquility*, and left it to melt and fill the crater.

I opted out early and grabbed an opportunity to monitor *Tranquility*. It meant I spent all my free time with Mary-Lou, which was just what I wanted, and I took a claim right on the water's edge. We built a cabin from imported Earth-wood: I even constructed a wooden dinghy, and for a while it served as my transport for Lunar Enterprises while I monitored the conditions at *Tranquility* and *Serenity*. That was before the company played god.

I watched the company fill *Tranquility* with aquatic creatures, but it was mainly the freshwater fish that survived: cod, redfin, carp, and dhobi.

Right about then many of the miners grew old before their time: they shriveled, their skin dried up. Many died far too young. The company knew something about it, or else they wouldn't have stopped cutting ice for *Serenity*: they never filled her to capacity.

Ice-miners departed with their families, they took their chances with Earth's poisoned oceans.

I stayed, perhaps they had blessed me with good health but I guessed it was because I hadn't mined as deep into the ice as some other men.

And something else I'd never mentioned. I'd rowed out on *Tranquility* in my wooden dinghy, to test the water quality, and spend some time fishing.

I'd stopped, like always, when I could see the distant structure of the spaceport between the small trees on the foreshore and threw out my line. Sunlight filtered through the thick dome and caught on the ripples from my dingy. It glistened in time with the hypnotic ebb and flow of the surface water.

Nearby, a bubble of foam burst from the surface and settled in a small ring. I thought it might have been expelled fish air, or fish spawn, but it changed into a hexagonal shape and firmed.

I rowed closer, grabbed my snorkel and goggles, and pulled them down over my head. I clambered to the side, holding a sample container.

The dinghy pitched back and forth, but I ignored it and leaned further over the side, forcing my head and shoulders into the cool water. Under the surface the hexagonal shape extended as a cloudy mass into the darkness below.

I reached forward with the sample container toward the cloudy mass.

It moved away.

Odd.

I leaned further out, balanced myself on the edge of the dinghy, and thrust the container deep into the heart of the mass for a sample.

It moved again, deeper this time, further out of reach.

I struggled to collect some and slid into the water, but I resisted the temptation to follow it deeper and clambered back topside.

Back in the dingy I searched the water's surface, but I found nothing. I scratched my head. Had I really seen a hexagonal shape? I couldn't be sure, but I decided not to tell anyone.

THE MOON WILL WANE gibbous tonight. The sunset line, or the terminator as we call her, sweeps slowly across *Tranquility's* dome. Even with the dome's protection, I fear it isn't enough. I've just learned that unexplained hexagon-shaped lines have appeared within the lining of the Dome, and I shiver as the first kiss of night touches. Below *Tranquility*, one of my favorite craters, *Theophilus*, with its central peak stands out from the shadows. Daylight fades as the fourteen-day night begins.

I look across the sweet beauty that is *Tranquility* and understand that she and *Serenity* are oceans apart when compared to Earth's poisoned oceans. Perhaps that is a good thing, and only time will tell, but now I saw *something* out on *Tranquility*, that day in my boat: I think it had to be the moon's soul, mined from deep within her, only to escape from the oceans, and so very much alive.

LATHAM'S STORY: SEA OF TRANQUILITY

The *Sea of Tranquility* is neither a veritable sea nor a tranquil place, although we tried to make it both.

I have my grandfather, Grantham, to thank. He and those brave men like him who had dreamed of creating a world in the image of Earth before much of their world dried up. Ice miners who toiled at the moon's poles once the domes over *Tranquility* and *Serenity* were constructed.

I'm glad none of them are alive to see it now, to learn about the city that grew from deep beneath *Tranquility's* dust. Perhaps the embryo of our ancestors has a unique view on time than we do and elicits a different response. Once liberated from the ice they ignored us, but not the things we made, not the things we relied on.

There is much I don't know, on the assumptions made about what happened in the billion years or so of the moon's existence. Who could have known that when that exo-planetary body plunged into the Earth, it contained the seeds of life? Too late, I say. But like *Tranquility* and the virus within it, the moon neither cares nor forgives.

FROM INSIDE MY HOME, I lift a withered, leathery arm and push myself from the chair. I struggle over to the window and look out at my vegetable patch. I see my spring onions... my shoulders fall. Recently, I had laid them down on the ground, with their frail white roots half exposed to the scorching sun's rays under the dome. I'd expected the automatic misters to feed them, have them take hold of the soil, and stand, and grow, but they haven't, and they kneel wilted, all twisted and grotesque. Contorted and bronze doesn't describe them. I understand their tenuous struggle to hold on to life.

The celery is the same, as too are the sprouts. The only one doing well is the Goji Berry bush, and it excelled with a giant flush of fruit berries, or so I thought, but each one looked like a miniature faceted city of bronze. I dare not eat them, or they may consume me.

I want to help them, but I dare not go out. Whatever has affected them has touched me too. I look at my arms and disappointment fill me. I haven't had the courage to look at my face, but I run my leathery fingers across my face and I know my face is much worse.

MY JOB IS TO MONITOR the Dome, and I like my isolation from the principal towns, so remote across on the other side of *Tranquility*. But now fear stops me from leaving the house. The dome is so thin, it could fail at any moment, and it's the daylight period. The temperatures outside the dome hover around one hundred Celsius. I can't go out. The night period approaches though, when temperatures fall to minus one hundred and seventy and below. Perhaps during transition, that four-hour window where temperatures moved from unbearable hot to freezing cold, I might be safe enough in my moon suit if the dome fails. I stare out the window to my mutant vegetables once again. I'm torn, frozen with indecision. Anxiety builds within me like a dormant volcano about to explode.

I CAN'T DO THIS. I can't sit and do nothing. The dome thins each day, and it won't be long now before it gives way. I can't stare out the window, while my body withers a little more each day. Inactivity will be the death of me. The communication systems are down. The virus eats everything we have. Our technology fails one by one. I must see Martha over at Serenity. See how she's doing. See if she needs a hand.

I throw on my moon suit, and my moon shoes, which look like snowshoes, but finer. They'll help me get cross-country to where the Dome that covers the *Sea of Serenity* meets the *Tranquility* Dome.

I BANG ON MARTHA'S door, and she opens it. I'm not surprised by her face when she opens the door, hers is as withered as mine but the runes are deeper. She struggles with a forlorn smile and steps aside so I can enter.

"Cup of tea?" she asks.

I nod and remove my helmet. She chuckles, "I thought it was just me," and she heads into the kitchen.

She returns with some tea, and we sit at her kitchen table. I tell her what little I've learned about the water-borne virus. I tell her I don't want to go to *Tranquility* Base, or to *Serenity*, neither of the big cities are for me.

She agrees and asks, "How long before—"

I hold up my hand. I shrug. "Anytime from my measurements. What do yours say?"

She shrugs. "The same. What should we do?"

"We should go on a holiday," I said and laughed. It felt good to laugh, I mean *really* laugh.

"Where?" she asks.

"The sea, where else."

She chews on her lip, and finally, nods. "Which one? The colorful one?"

"Ah," I nod. She means *Tranquility*. "Are you up for the trek?" I ask.

She nods again. "Better go before the darkness."

I frown and then smile, but I wonder which darkness she is referring to.

She stands and picks up my empty cup. "I'll just pack a few things, and get my new swimming costume," she says.

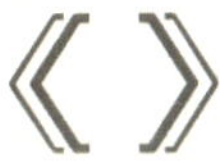

I DRAG THE SUN BEDS off my porch and across the dusty soil toward the *Sea of Tranquility*. It's an effort, I've no strength left, and I'm sweating by the time I reach the water's edge.

Martha stands there, watching. She's such a lady, and I am happy that she didn't help and allowed me to wait on her. I have to admit, that in her blue two-piece bikini, she still looks mighty fine, even if her skin is like dried beef jerky.

"Did you check?" she asks.

I nod. I know she's referring to the thickness of *Tranquility's* Dome. "When?"

"Soon," It's all I can say. I have little moisture inside me left to swallow.

We embrace and sit on our sun beds.

"It's pretty," she says.

I turn and stare out at the freshwater sea. The *Sea of Tranquility* that has been my home since I was a boy.

I have to admire them, the virus and how it has manifested. The new structure it built seems to take on a life of its own, it's growing in height every day, and I think I can make out windows in the multi-faceted structure.

I'm not sure what will give first. I'm not sure if the Dome will thin enough as the virus attacks it and break, or if the city that grows out of the sea will pierce the Dome first. Either way, I cannot do anything. I've run out of fight.

I lean in and dip two glasses into the water teeming with a different life, and lean back to my sun bed. I offer the second glass to Martha and imagine I'm holidaying on the south of France. We sip on the water and watch the construction of the alien city with distant interest. Pain racks my withered body, and I raise my glass one last time and toast Grandfather.

I think he'd be proud to know I spent my last moments enjoying his legacy.

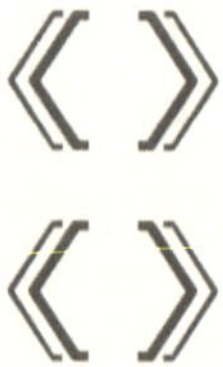

PART III: TERRAFORMING VENUS

THE FIRST LAW OF HAVOC: FALLING BETWEEN SECONDS

The first law of thermodynamics, also known as the *Law of Conservation of Energy*, states that energy cannot be created or destroyed in an isolated system. And Abe knew the Earth was a closed system, right? At least for his sake, he hoped so…

Abe's hands shook as he closed his suit helmet. After, he would tell his granddaughter, Lucy, to count every moment as her last. To live between the seconds of time and take notice of those fleeting moments: that was what life was really about.

"Ready?"

Abe nodded to the man tightening his harness straps and held up his hand as they bit into his carbon-reinforced jumpsuit. He took a deep breath. His heart pounded louder than he could remember. At this point, everything that might be, anything that could be, and everything that would be was in the hands of the gods. He couldn't turn back even if he wanted. Pride was a powerful emotion. The thought made Abe's palms sweat. He chewed his lip. Was it too late to reconsider?

He thrust the thought aside as the intercontinental jump vessel kicked off and accelerated high into the sky. Vertigo couldn't describe it.

They say a hundred is the new fifty. Abe hoped them right, but wasn't sure if he could live up to it. He weighed the negatives: no warm, loving body to lie with at night, nobody to smile at when the blue wrens flew into the back garden at the onset of winter. Nobody to share life's simple mindless moments. Hell, he shouldn't have been here, but the emergency team had been lightning quick to resuscitate him after his heart attack. He didn't deserve to have survived his wife's death. What was the point of being at all?

Okay. Maybe this was training for a higher cause. Perhaps he'd be successful in being part of the proposed High-Altitude Venus Operational Craft, HAVOC. If so, this jump was good training.

Abe fought vertigo as the wind forces buffeted him, testing the straps that bound his jettison pod to the outside of the vessel.

Below, the launch site seemed small, alien, and the many people on the ground swarmed like a billion tiny ants. His car grew smaller with every passing second until it too was an ant. And then a speck of sand.

Back in 2060, the third prophet to appear in that century reminded the world that only in death can we really feel life. Abe agreed, but his knees still shook, and his stomach couldn't tighten any further. What was the worst that could happen? He'd find out soon enough.

Abe's only regret was that he'd forgotten to will all his assets to his granddaughter. Not that she'd be interested enough to flick through the faded photographs, the poorly made videos, or the virtual info movies he'd placed himself in.

Earlier, the idea of free-falling from the edge of the planet's atmosphere had sounded like fun. Now, doubt knotted his stomach.

He checked the straps of his parachute and the oxygen pack, ensured they were tight against his form-fit bodysuit and heat shield.

The suit was designed to slow him, repair itself in freefall with a million or more nanobots tending to every blemish in the suit's surface. He grimaced. He couldn't be in better hands.

"Ready yourself!" The voice sounded thin through his earpiece. He swallowed hard and reminded himself he'd already died once.

The jump station towers below had faded into insignificance. Like him.

An alarm went off in his earpiece. The peak of the vessel's trajectory was ten seconds away. If he was going to, it was time to jump.

He bit down on the corner of his mouth and unclipped his safety harness. His heart galloped in his chest and ears. Abe raised his arms up into a point above him and breathed in. "Check," he said. Another thing achieved on his bucket list.

A heat shield would engage. The pod would jettison. Three parachutes would deploy automatically and mark his descent to those on the ground. But initially, he could free-fall. Free of the world.

The earphone crackled. "This is your captain speaking. If you look out the starboard side of the aircraft, you can wave goodbye as our braver customer, Abe, who decided to cut his flight a little short today."

Abe tried to wave, released the final restraint, and jumped.

What a rush! He wanted to vomit and laugh at the same time. Dizzy beyond his expectations, exhilarating didn't begin to describe it.

Abe twisted his head. Above him, in the cruising intercontinental vehicle, he caught a glimpse of somebody waving. He grinned. Below him, everything seemed immense. He felt insignificant, and pressed his arms to his sides. Like a bullet, he fell and sped toward the ground.

He pushed self-doubt, and the vision of his suit ripping apart, aside. His fists tightened like rocks, but he forced himself to enjoy every sickening moment between the seconds and tried not to think of death.

In the time it'd take him to travel to Earth's surface, another ten thousand people would be born. Nine thousand would die. That was a thousand more mouths to feed and to divide the dwindling fresh water supply between. More potential neighbour disputes over boundary fences. More babies in prams hogging footpaths and train entrances. Each wanting a dog or two cats.

The pod jettisoned. Abe lurched from the sky with his heart in his throat, speechless and giddy beyond belief. He wanted to die all over again. He sighed, but in free-fall, it sounded like a dog growling under its breath. Up here, right now, none of that seemed relevant. For a moment, everything settled. The Earth looked beautiful. Giant rivers ran like blue veins across a wrinkly giant's mottled skin.

He could see the deserts where cloud seeding had failed, and people were without water. To his right was an area of white gold: former cotton plantations. Where precious water had been dammed to grow cotton and watercourses changed. Where once water-rich green landscapes had died along with the cotton and humankind.

An alarm went off in his earpiece again, this one warning him of the first parachute. He took a breath and braced himself for the first gut-wrenching jolt.

Nothing happened. Abe's pulse raced. He didn't slow. He counted off the seconds, jettisoned the first parachute and grimaced in concern. It'd be a rough landing, but he'd faced worse in the military.

Before when he'd died, and they revived him, he'd never thought about a bucket list, about pushing himself into situations where he was out of his comfort zone. Like this one.

The ground grew closer, the mottled green giant replaced with pockets of green and blue. The tarmac bigger, harder.

Another alarm buzzed. Sooner than Abe had expected, but he was free-falling faster, and further, than planned. This chute would hurt.

He braced himself for the body-jarring thump as the parachute's sails filled, but again, nothing happened, and he continued to free-fall toward the ground.

He jettisoned the second of the three parachutes and chewed his lip.

Panic wouldn't help, he reminded himself. The final chute would engage, and he'd float gently down to the ground. Well not gently, he'd probably break a leg or two, perhaps a pelvis, but that was later, and everything was out of his hands. He could choose to accept the giddy sensation as the ground grew larger below him, to enjoy those moments between time. After all, he couldn't complain. Before he had died, there had been plenty of time to do the things he wanted—one day—and that day had come and gone. This was his second chance.

He pushed open his arms to slow himself, opened his legs—just enough to create more drag—and and his body shuddered. Too fast.

Buzz.

The trees and hills loomed large. He braced. If the last chute would have been body-jolting, this one would almost be a killer. Four...three...two...one...

Nothing happened.

The chute failed. Abe cringed and jettisoned it.

He stared at the ground and manoeuvred toward a canopy of trees.

He recalled what was next on his bucket list. He'd begin planning that hike up the Himalaya's, feeling thin air chill his lungs. He'd have to do some training, some hill climbs, if he was lucky enough before HAVOC—

He reached the first of the highest leaves and crashed into the canopy. Tree branches snapped, and he continued to fall. Who knew? He could do it all again tomorrow...live between the seconds in time. Like he had today...if he survived...

THE SECOND LAW OF HAVOC: FLOATING IN ACID

The second law of thermodynamics states that the entropy of an isolated system always increases. This meant that the Venetian atmosphere would invariably become more disorderly in time as more High-Altitude Venus Operational Crafts were deployed. HAVOC! Abe hoped so. Who knew what might happen as a result?

Aboard *Sycamore-50*, one of the thousand 200-meter-long Zeppelins, Abe nursed his repaired pelvis. His hand moved to his ribs, where eight of them had mended in flight to Venus. A couple were still sore. But falling from the earth's outer atmosphere without a parachute can do that to a person.

Abe watched the cloud seeding ejectile disperse from the rear of his zeppelin. Perhaps they could change the albedo of the planet and cool the thick atmosphere. There were enough zeppelins in formation across the planet to try. Imagine if they could cool the planet's atmosphere and make it more habitable. He gripped the deployment controller with his other hand and readied himself, leaned forward inside the viewing platform and looked down at the sea of acid cloud formations around him. It was almost like he was the captain of an old sailing ship, bobbing up and down as he sailed the high seas to new worlds. Except this was the New World. And this ocean was mostly carbon dioxide and sulfuric acid. Water and oxygen were scarce.

Above the giant helium-filled balloon, an array of solar panels powered the zeppelin. Each zeppelin had a towed mini pontoon with a tree growing from it. Behind them were a vast array of trees: boabs, cacti, oaks, strawberry clover, and beeches. Abe's was a sycamore, floating 50 kilometres above the surface of the planet where conditions were similar to earth. Except for the heat, and the empty oceans, and the glorious earth sunrises.

Excitement built within Abe as he approached the continent-sized uplands of Ishtar Terra, slightly east of Ishtar's highest mountain plateau. Maxwell Montes approached! At eleven kilometers above the planet's surface, it was the closest point to him, which meant earth's oxygen-producing bacteria had better conditions to survive

Abe tensed. He leaned forward and watched for a slight break between the clouds below and counted backward from five. The Zeppelin shook from the turbulence caused by the hot Venetian air forced up from its surface. He steadied himself and pressed the deployment button. Another series of bio-matter pods launched and descended through the clouds to begin their 39-kilometre journey to the highest surface of Venus

He hoped for a cataclysmic combination...

All going well, the microbes would descend into the coldest part of the Venetian surface and convert the acidic climate to one where oxygen creating microbes excelled.

He hoped it would only be a matter of time before the planet was habitable. Where every few years they planned to lower the zeppelins as the planet's atmosphere cooled. The trees would help. Adding terrestrial bio-matter and seeding the clouds is all they could do. Earth was on borrowed time. Perhaps this terraformed Venus could be the New Earth... and maybe chaos would eventuate like it had there a millennium ago, and the second law of thermodynamics would hold true. Who new? They could only try for humankind.

THE THIRD LAW OF HAVOC: THE NEW ANTIPODES

The third law of thermodynamics states that the entropy of a system approaches a constant value as the temperature approaches absolute zero. This wasn't going to be the case for Venus, even if Kevin's grandfather, Abe, an early coloniser had helped the temperature of planet's atmosphere drop. Today, just over a million people lived in a connected network of five smaller colonies: the New Antipodes, but not everyone was happy.

Kevin's chest tightened. His finger hovered over his zeppelin's firing mechanism, and he throttled the zeppelin forward through the thick sulfuric fog so that spotlights moved across the ancient colony tree known as Sycamore 50. This tree was one of the many that had been successfully been transplanted into the terraformed Venusian soil. Many of these ancient trees still grew and oxygenated the planet, but those opposed to a more earth-like Venus, resisted and threatened the trees for their role in transforming the world.

The zeppelin's radar screen lit. Several High-Altitude Venus Operational Crafts, HAVOC's appeared in the habitable zone above him. Kevin examined their radar tracks to ensure they were all friendlies, but one jittered and set off in an odd track toward an ancient boab.

Kevin armed a heat-sinking missile and studied the track. Finger on the trigger, he paused. Was this all that life had been reduced to? A distant contact and button presses before he extinguished life?

He couldn't do it.

Chaos theory said that something good would come of varied opinions.

He took a breath and the contact faded. Still, doubt gnawed at his conscience. What if it was an anti-earth colonist.

He feathered his zeppelin forward toward the dark corner of the ancient tree and an object slid into the shadows.

Bright light stained the back of his retinas. Something struck the zeppelin's inner metal core.

When he opened his eyes, the communications status glowed red and an alarm sounded.

Kevin's hand tightened on the controls. He returned fired, careful to avoid the giant tree. He missed and fired again. The rogue vessel, a smaller dark zeppelin, glowed. Yes! He smiled, but that changed as the other vessel released twin missiles.

Kevin grimaced. There was nothing to do except brace. His zeppelin shuddered, tilted sideways as the gas evacuated from its skin. Cabin lights extinguished and green emergency beacons glowed.

The zeppelin fell. The other followed him into the crushing depths of the poisonous Venusian atmosphere.

It fired at him and light flashed around him. He aimed his sights to fire but the other zeppelin deployed a parachute and vanished from sight as Kevin continued to fall.

Adrenalin coursed through him. He activated his parachute and braced for the gut-wrenching jerk. Nothing happened except the zeppelin fell faster. A high external pressure alarm screamed. The zeppelin's small inner hull groaned.

He pulled the seat straps tight and activated the backup parachute to stop his descent. He braced, his stomach tight as he counted down the seconds from five.

Nothing.

Outside the atmosphere had turned thick and darkness greeted. Small mountains of frozen sulphuric acid threatened. The zeppelin's inner metal walls twisted and groaned.

He ripped the seat straps off and scurried to the rear, wide-eyed. He yanked open a torpedo hatch, and climbed into the fortified metal coffin feet first. His heart pounded loud in his ears. Kevin wiped his sweaty palms dry on his clothes and reached above him. He pulled the hatch door closed and in the darkness screwed it shut. The stale air made him gag. He braced his knees against the sides of the freezing metal, pressed his shoulder against one side and tucked his chin against his chest. His left palm covered the red glow of the launch button. He took what might be his last breath and held it, pressed the button and braced. Outside shaped charges exploded and the metal vessel shuddered. It jerked upright and Kevin closed his eyes and counted the seconds between time as the missile launched itself toward the outer atmosphere of Venus.

What could go wrong? The laws of thermodynamics were on his side. Why else had his grandfather designed this failsafe? But part of him what would happen if he struck the New Antipodes colony.

RACING IN THE MURKS

Gossamer thin strands of grapheme-coated titanium were all that separated Mike from death. They connected his zeppelin, the *MV Endeavour*, to its gas-filled membrane and kept him afloat in the thick sulphuric clouds. Mike tilted the ship, so it angled deep into the lowest depths of the Murks of Venus.

Across his bow, Jim from the *Tardigrade* was doing the same. A cylinder-like airship not too dissimilar from his own, its balloon wires were also taut against the impossible downward angle. Mike examined his competitor's angle of descent and cursed. He took a deep breath, tightened his grip on the helm until his knuckles whitened. Dare he tilt his ship even further? In the end, he did and cursed again when *Tardigrade* followed suit.

The radio burst into life. "Five, four, three, two, one, go." He throttled his engines and felt the tug of the thin strands of titanium against the inflated balloon above him.

Mike held his breath. Launching deep into The Murks could be hit and miss and nobody wanted to tear the delicate strands holding their only lifeline, preventing them from spiralling indefinitely into the Venusian surface.

The radio crackled again. "God speed, *Endeavour*. God speed, *Tardigrade*."

Mike exhaled. The altimeter measured a slow but increasing declination. He grinned, counted down from ten, and glanced across to the *Tardigrade*. He cursed. Although a distance apart, both ships were neck and neck.

Why did he have such a desire to prove himself? Was it ego? Fame? Or purely about terraforming Venus? Probably a little of everything. Yes, he wanted to be a famous explorer like his grandfather, Abe. Yes, like the *Tardigrade* was known for releasing water monkeys into the depths of the Murks, Mike had a reputation for releasing the mycelium from his onboard mushroom farm. Call him eccentric. He didn't mind. Maybe there was a bit of ego there, too.

He would always navigate the ship close to the equator so he could cross the edge of Venus's largest continental plate, *Aphrodite Terra*. He'd sail among the toxic sulphuric acid clouds until he found the roasting volcanic thermal vent currents and release the mycelium into it, hoping it mixed in the primordial soup that harboured the basic building blocks of life. The Venusian Goldilocks zone.

Mike found the thermal vent plume and sailed on its edge. Perspiration formed across his forehead. He checked his pressure gauge. While higher than he'd like, he could go a little further, but the ship was warming down at this level.

The *Tardigrade* sailed slightly below him, and Mike cursed. Jim was going to beat him. He held the line for longer and counted down from ten. With each passing second, the temperature inside grew. At the count of five, the temperature was uncomfortable, and the atmosphere so thick outside, the *Tardigrade* was barely visible.

Four, three... At two the *Tardigrade* changed her trajectory, and flattened her incline. The *MV Endeavour* shot passed her, deeper into The Murks, and Mike cheered. He had won.

The radio crackled into life. "Way to go, *Endeavour*. I'll see you topside, Mike," said Jim.

Mike reached for the radio, but something drove him on. The *MV Endeavour* was a military vessel. She had been built as a warship, and Mike needed to see how deeper she could go.

He slowed his descent, and feathered the controls so that the ship sat off to the side of the thermal vent plume, at a position where the air temperature was slightly cooler and the external pressure less.

He chased the heat plume deeper into The Murks, uncertain how much further his vessel could withstand. According to his depth gauge, he was the first human to have gone this far into the depths of Venus. He checked the pressure gauge and considered going down even further, but decided against it. This was his limit.

He pulled up *Endeavour*, positioned her for the return topside journey, but the titanium cables caught on something. They snapped. He cursed loudly and watched the balloon shoot up into the distance, while he sped down faster into the crushing maws of Venus.

He frowned. What had she snagged on? Quickly, he replayed the external video feed while he still could.

He frowned again, and it deepened. What was he looking at? It seemed to be a replica of an early Spanish sailing ship, but instead of a central mast and sails, the cylindrical hull had huge spreading mushrooms instead, and the gills moved back and forth like a fish.

Mike grinned. He couldn't believe it. Could he have something to do with that, after all? Or had life spawned with the help of Jim Banks' Tardigrades? Had it simply been microbes brought from Earth on the trees? Or that the poisonous clouds above the giant continental plate, *Aphrodite Terra*, contained the basic building blocks for life? It didn't matter now.

Content, he sat back in his chair, closed his eyes, and slowly counted down from one hundred as he went. He had no regrets, except one, and that was he would take this knowledge of life on Venus to his grave.

Fortunately, he passed out before he reached zero, which is when the massive Venusian pressure would crush the *MV Endeavour*, and him with it, to death.

EPILOGUE

BEFORE JIM BANKS HAD arrived topside, he had reported Mike's death and losing the *MV Endeavour*. From the deck of the *Tardigrade*, Jim had watched *Endeavour's* balloon pass him, and sadly knew the worst of it. Jim and Mike had been great friends and rivals, after all.

Topside, where the traditional colonists bounced above The Murks in their High-Altitude Venus Operational Crafts, the HAVOCs, they still pulled the ancient Earth trees of the early colonists behind them to increase the oxygen levels.

Jim organised a funeral for Mike. Out of respect for the person who had travelled the deepest into The Murks of Venus. Jim offered to sponsor a new seedling to be delivered from Earth, so that it could be towed behind Mike's grandfather's sycamore tree.

Everyone topside thought it was a wonderful gesture, but it never came to pass because Mike returned in a changed *MV Endeavour*. The outside hull of the ship had been coated in a thick layer of buoyant mycelium, and now she looked like an ancient Spanish galleon but with mushroom sails.

END

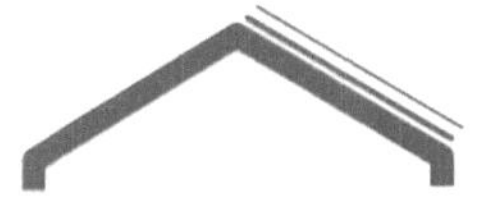

ACKNOWLEDGEMENTS

Gaia's Virus was first published by AntipodeanSF in Issue 60, October 2011.

Gaia's Legacy was first published by Timid Pirates Publishing and appeared in their Finding Home: Community in Apocalyptic Worlds Anthology in November 2011

The First Law Of Havoc: Falling Between Second, was first published by AntipodeanSF in Issue 250, May 2019

The Second Law Of Havoc: Floating In Acid, was first published by AntipodeanSF in Issue 252, September 2019

The Third Law Of Havoc: The New Antipodes, was first published by AntipodeanSF in Issue 261, June 2020

Racing in the Murks was first published by AntipodeanSF in Issue 306, April 2024

Don't miss out!

Visit the website below and you can sign up to receive emails whenever David Kernot publishes a new book. There's no charge and no obligation.

https://books2read.com/r/B-A-LKNUD-KVLHG

BOOKS 2 READ

Connecting independent readers to independent writers.

Did you love *Panspermian Earth*? Then you should read *Future Worlds*[1] by David Kernot!

[2]

A collection of five novelette length stories that highlight mankind's exploration of the universe, and the struggle to live among the stars, of the hope of finding new and future worlds.

Read more at www.davidkernot.com.

---

1. https://books2read.com/u/bQw8M6

2. https://books2read.com/u/bQw8M6

Also by David Kernot

Beam Rider
The Early Years
Autumn Comes Slowly
Panspermian Earth
The Search for Giselle
Future Worlds
Gateway Through Time
Not Like Us

Watch for more at www.davidkernot.com.

About the Author

David Kernot is an Australian author living in the Mid North of South Australia. He writes contemporary fantasy, science and climate fiction, and horror, and is the author of over eighty published short stories in a variety of anthologies in Australia, the US, Canada, and the UK including the Year's Best Australian Fantasy & Horror, and Award Winning Australian Writing. He released his first dark sci-fi indie novel, Gateway Through Time in 2020. It joins a 2024 novella, Nor Like Us, two novelettes and five collections of short fiction. More information can be found at http://www.davidkernot.com

Read more at www.davidkernot.com.